THE FAIRY WINGS

Arctic Fox Rescue

Written and illustrated by

Marisa Peña

SNOWDROP
BOOKS

* A Fairy World Book *

Redmond, Washington

SNOWY MEADOWS

Cloud Top
Mountain

Snowy Owl
Village

Snow Haven

Cascade
Range

Springtime Sea
Mossy Vale
Feather Cliffs
Fox Tail Hollow
Hoof Print Glade
Puffin Beak
N
W
E
S

This book is dedicated to the Arctic.

ISBN 978-1-960834-00-3 (paperback)

ISBN 978-1-960834-01-0 (hardcover)

ISBN 978-1-960834-02-7 (e-book)

LCCN 2023915594

www.snowdropbooks.com

Printed in the United States of America

Written and illustrated by Marisa Peña

Cover design by Jenny Rez

Cover art by Marisa Peña

TABLE OF CONTENTS

CHAPTER 1
THE CEREMONY

It was the last day of summer in Snowy Meadows. The Arctic snow and ice had melted. The ground was lively shades of green and brown. Blankets of cotton grass swayed in the breeze.

On days like this, North loved to climb over the mossy rocks, fly around the misty waterfalls, and explore the new tunnels.

But today was different. She had a very important place to be. She was at the Autumn Celebration held by the Arctic Fairy Queen.

North was sitting with three other fairies. It was one of the most important days of their lives. Today, they were becoming Frost Wings.

An orchestra played a song as everyone settled into their seats. North was feeling restless and excited. *What will the Arctic Fairy Queen say? What roles will she give us?* she wondered.

North did not know the other Frost
Wings. They must have come from
different fairy villages.

They had a little time together
before the ceremony started.

That's when she met Lucy.

Lucy had red hair. She seemed to
know so many interesting things about
the Arctic. North already learned from
her that snow geese like to eat the
cotton grass that was growing nearby.

North also briefly met Charm.

Charm had two long black braids. She wore a green dress the color of tundra moss.

Before the ceremony, Charm spent time gathering cotton grass. By the time the ceremony began, she had already woven the grass into a crown.

North also met Willow. Willow had a cloud of black hair that rose off her head in tight ringlets and spirals.

North talked to Willow a little before the ceremony, but Willow did not say a lot. She seemed a little shy. And now that the ceremony had started, she seemed to be especially nervous. She was taking deep breaths.

When the fairy musicians were done playing the opening song, the Arctic Fairy Queen walked to the center of the willow birch arena.

She had long hair. It blew in the breezes that swirled around her. She wore a flowing dress in various shades of blue and green.

"Welcome, Fairies," the queen said. "Today we celebrate the change of seasons. It is also a special day for the Arctic fairy world. Today, we welcome our new team of Frost Wings. They will live and work together to help the animals of the tundra."

"Fairies, I will call each of you forward," the queen explained. "You will receive your Frost Wings role, and I will grant you special magical powers."

Each fairy took a deep breath.

"North Everstar, please step forward," said the queen.

CHAPTER 2

MAGICAL POWERS

North walked to the queen and knelt before her. The queen placed her magical hand on North's head. North felt a bubbling energy travel through her whole body. She suddenly had vivid memories of all the beautiful places she had explored.

Misty waterfalls.

Icicle-filled snow caves.

Fields of wildflowers.

"North, I sense your adventurous spirit and knowledge of the land. I grant you the powers of a Frost Wings Navigator," the queen said.

North's wings joyfully flew open. She looked at the queen with a beaming smile.

"I am presenting you with a magical bow and arrow," the queen continued. "There are various arrows in your quiver. They can do amazing things."

"Thank you," said North, who bowed in gratitude. She returned to her seat, holding her new bow. She wore the quiver of arrows on her back. The smooth wood in her hands felt amazing. She never wanted to let it go.

"Charm Iceglade, please step forward," said the queen.

Charm felt like she was walking in a dream. The setting sun was lighting up the billowy tops of the cotton grass. Everything seemed to be glowing.

She knelt before the queen. She felt the queen's hand on her head. She suddenly had vivid memories of all the things she had made in her life.

Baskets woven in the shapes of whales.

Costumes for village children.

Fancy chairs for her grandparents.

"Charm, I sense your outstanding crafting skills. I grant you the powers of a Frost Wings Maker," said the queen. "And in your first year as a Frost Wing, you shall have The Power of Magical Sewing."

Charm's face was beaming with joy. The queen presented her with a beautiful box. She opened the top. She saw a sparkling thread resting on a bed of green moss. The thread shimmered with rainbow colors in the light.

"That is a Magic Thread," the queen explained. "It will enchant whatever item you choose to make with it."

Charm bowed to the queen and thanked her. Then she walked back to her seat, holding this new treasure in her hands.

"Lucy Dawn, please step forward," said the Arctic queen.

The queen placed her hand on Lucy's head.

Then a strange, silly feeling came over Lucy. It was not a feeling she expected at this serious moment! Playful pictures of adorably cute animals flashed through her mind.

Baby harp seals with their fluffy white fur and big brown eyes.

A young wobbly reindeer just learning to walk.

Baby birds with their beaks open, waiting for food.

Lucy started to giggle and melt right there in front of the queen!

"Lucy, I sense your deep love of animals. I grant you the powers of a Frost Wings Healer. In your first year as a Frost Wing, you will have the ability to magically heal small injuries."

"And as a special gift," the queen continued, "I am presenting you with a set of books. They are about the plants and animals of the Arctic."

Lucy was overjoyed. She bowed and thanked the queen. She walked back to her seat and gave an encouraging smile to Willow.

"Willow Brightfrost, please step forward," said the queen.

Willow walked nervously toward her. *Was I really meant to be here?* she thought. *What role can I possibly be?*

Willow spent most of her childhood helping her younger brother and sister. They were older now and didn't need her help as much anymore.

Her parents encouraged her to follow her heart's wish to see places beyond her village. So, Willow volunteered for the Arctic Fairy Queen's organization. But she thought she would get a simple job. She was stunned when the queen asked her to be a Frost Wing.

Willow knelt in front of the queen. The queen placed her hand on Willow's head. A warm and cozy feeling filled Willow's body. Loving memories of her family filled her mind.

Seeing her little brother's huge smile when she helped him learn to fly.

Getting a love note from her little sister.

Telling her little sister bedtime stories when she couldn't fall asleep.

"Willow, I sense your kindness and your empathy. I grant you the powers of a Frost Wings Spellcaster," said the queen.

Willow thought the queen must have made a mistake. *A Spellcaster? Wasn't that a big power? Shouldn't that be for the brave and bold? Not someone cautious and quiet like me!* she thought.

Willow looked at the queen with a puzzled expression. The queen seemed to read her thoughts.

"Willow, there are many kinds of strength and courage," the queen said. "I only give the Spellcaster role to the most compassionate fairies. I know that you will use these strong powers for the good of the tundra. You are receiving spells of fire, ice, water, wind, and earth."

Tears of surprise and gratitude filled Willow's eyes as she received a magic wand from the queen.

Willow floated back to her teammates, smiling back at all of them.

As the sun set, the golden light filled the arena. North, Lucy, Charm, and Willow felt the sun on their backs. Their new life as Frost Wings was about to begin.

CHAPTER 3
SNOW DAY

The Frost Wings spent the next few weeks of autumn practicing their new magical powers. They settled into Snow Haven, their Arctic home.

Today they were playing outside. Freshly fallen snow covered the land. It was glittering in the sunlight.

Lucy was laying on her back and wiggling. She was trying to press her fairy wings deep into the snow.

Somehow, North could always get Lucy out of a cozy and warm reading chair and into an outdoor activity. With North, Lucy usually ended up either wet, cold, or dirty. That was North's idea of a great time.

"That's it, Lucy!" North cheered. "Now fly straight up and look at your flower print! I'll walk in a straight line and make the stem!"

Lucy flew up into the sky. She looked down at the flower they made. "Wow, that looks like a Tundra Rose!" she exclaimed. "It looks great!"

Lucy felt the frost on her wings. She was shivering. But it brought a huge smile to her face.

Nearby, Willow and Charm were building a snow narwahl. They used an icicle for the horn.

Then the fairies heard a special twinkling in the air. It was coming from the enchanted wind chimes outside their home. It only made that sound when the queen was calling.

CHAPTER 4
MESSAGE FROM THE QUEEN

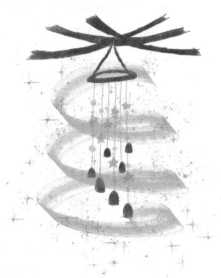

The Frost Wings gathered around the twinkling wind chimes.

A ribbon of sparkling air swirled around the chimes. Then it swirled around the Frost Wings. It gave them goosebumps! They could hear the Arctic Fairy Queen's voice speaking to them from this ribbon of enchanted air!

"Hello, Frost Wings," said the queen. "A very young fox needs your help. He is stranded and alone on an ice floe. He was separated from his parents when the ice floe drifted away from the shore. Will you help him?"

"We certainly will, Your Highness," North replied.

"Very good," the queen said.

After a long pause, the queen continued in more serious tone. "I have another important matter to discuss with you. I have learned that Blaze has used fairy magic to enchant a crow. She  can now ride this crow to cover great distances in the sky. You will need to take extra care."

Blaze was once part of the royal court. Blaze grew envious of the Arctic Fairy Queen's power, so she turned against the queen.

The fairies knew to be careful of Blaze. Blaze might try to steal their magical items. She had already stolen several of the queen's magic gems.

"Thank you," responded North. "We will be careful."

"I am pleased to hear that," said the queen. "Fairies, I will not keep you any longer. There is not much time to find the fox before the sun goes down. He is to the west of you. To find him, fly in the direction of the setting sun."

After they said goodbye, the chimes stopped twinkling. The ribbon of air seemed to drift away.

North had spoken with so much
confidence. But as soon as the queen
was gone, she blew out the air she was
holding. She let the nervousness and
excitement show on her face.

The other fairies shared North's
feelings. It was their first mission as
Frost Wings. They all wanted to do a
good job.

CHAPTER 5
FLYING WEST

The fairies flew west, over a sea filled with ice floes. They carefully scanned each ice floe they passed, looking for the young fox.

It was getting colder. As they flew over the frosty sea, the frigid wind blew in their faces.

"Fairies, I can barely see through my frozen lashes!" North called out. "It is making this extra difficult!"

"Yes!" Lucy added. "And the fox will be very hard to spot against the snow. Their fur is so white this time of year. They match the snow almost perfectly!"

Willow was looking in the sky for any sign of Blaze.

North suddenly heard something unusual. She had the best hearing. She always heard important sounds before the others.

"Do you hear that?" North asked. "I think I hear a howl! Follow me!"

The fairies followed North, in the direction of the sound.

"I think I see him!" she shouted.

There, on a very small ice floe, they saw a small Arctic fox. Its two black eyes were the only thing they could see in the big blur of white fur and snow.

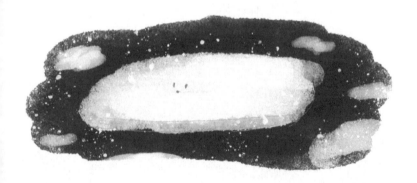

The fairies flew closer to the little fox. Upon seeing the fairies, the fox got nervous. He began to dig a hole in the snow to hide.

"Hello, Little Fox," Willow said. "We came to help you. You do not need to be afraid. We are your friends."

At the sound of her gentle voice, the fox stopped digging. He looked up at the fairies.

"Hello," he said. "I am scared. I want to go home."

"Don't worry, Little Fox. We will find a way to get you home," comforted Willow.

"What's your name?" asked Lucy.

"Pounce," he replied.

North thought she heard the fox's tummy rumble. "Are you hungry, Pounce?"

"Yes!" he eagerly replied.

North knew just what to do. She reached into her quiver and pulled out a magic arrow.

She held her bow up and pulled the arrow back. She pointed toward the sky and said the magic words.

Hunger strikes.
But no food to be found.
Show us a trail
To where good food abounds!

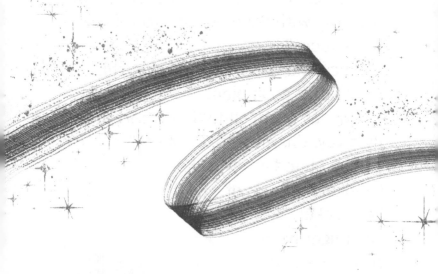

The arrow shot up into the air. It exploded into a glittering purple trail in the sky. Then the trail drifted away from them toward the shore.

CHAPTER 6
A GLITTERING TRAIL

North called to the other fairies. "I will follow the trail to find some food for Pounce."

"I can join you!" Willow offered. "Then we will be in teams of two. Two will stay with Pounce and two will get some food."

Lucy and Charm agreed that this would be a good plan.

Just as North and Willow started to fly away, Charm yelled, "Wait!"

She pulled a tiny, silken red handkerchief out of her pocket. "I think you might need this," she said.

Charm gave it to North. "If you find food, you might need something to carry it in."

"Good idea, Charm! Thank you!" North said. She put it in her pocket. Then the two fairies flew off in the direction of the sparkling air trail.

The air trail swirled and drifted through the sky. The fairies followed it to the shore. It led them to a cluster of big rocks covered in snow.

The purple trail curled up into a ball and exploded. It scattered purple glitter over a blank patch of snow. Then it promptly disappeared.

Willow was confused. "Why did the trail suddenly stop here on this bare patch of snow? I don't see any food around," she said.

North looked perplexed as well. But then her face suddenly brightened.

"Oh, I think I know why it stopped here!" North exclaimed. "Lucy told me that Arctic foxes will bury their food in the snow. That's how they keep it fresh in the winter. Let's try digging in that spot."

They began digging. But they were both getting quite cold. They were not making very good progress.

"I think a warmth spell could help us do this more quickly," Willow said.

She pulled out her wand.

CHAPTER 7
A WARMING GLOW

Willow said the magic words.

Warming light, from this wand I hold.
Melt the ice, warm the cold!

The wand created a red sparkling sphere that made its own heat. It hovered over the snow. As the snow melted, the fairies could see small pink balls poking through.

"Cloudberries!" cried North.

"Hooray!" cried Willow.

North pulled out the small, folded handkerchief that Charm had given her.

She unfolded it, and it got bigger. She unfolded it again. And again, and again. Every time she unfolded it, it magically got bigger!

She soon had a blanket of fabric big enough to hold all the berries.

As they gathered the berries, North's joy was cut short. She saw a dark figure in the sky. It was in the shape of a large crow in flight.

"Oh no, that might be Blaze!" said North.

North quickly pulled Willow into the crevice of a nearby rock.

The crow got closer to the fairies. It was unlike any crow they had ever seen. It had dark red feathers, glinting in the sunlight.

Blaze sat on top, dressed in a dark purple jacket with a tiara on her head. Her tiara held a huge red gem in the center. BLAZE was written in fancy, big letters on the riding blanket draped over the crow's back.

North and Willow were in a good hiding place. But they could see that their blanket of berries was out in plain sight! Blaze only had to turn her head in their direction to see it. Then she would know that they were nearby!

CHAPTER 8
A PILE OF SNOW

Willow noticed a large outcrop of snow covering an Arctic birch tree. It was bending over the berry pile. She pulled out her wand and whispered a spell.

A wind so strong. A wind so fast.
Time to blow! Time to blast!

A gust of strong wind bolted from
her wand. It blew into the birch,
shaking it strongly. All the snow that
was piled on top fell to the ground,
burying the berries and the blanket
under snow.

Blaze heard the drop of the snow pile. But by the time she turned her head to look at the source of the sound, she saw nothing but snow.

And so, she turned back around. She continued to fly in the other direction, away from the fairies.

"Phew!" gasped Willow.

"Yes, that was close!" said North.

"What a relief she's gone," Willow said. "At least for now. Let's hurry and get this food back to Pounce. The sun is starting to set."

Willow began melting the snow off the berries once again. That's when she noticed bird tracks in the snow.

"Look at those bird tracks, North!" she said. "Do you know what kind of bird makes those tracks?"

Willow knew North had a special talent at identifying animal tracks in the snow.

North studied the tracks.

"It's a Rock Ptarmigan," she said. "They are big birds! Maybe this bird can help us carry these berries. Let's follow those tracks!"

The fairies followed the tracks over a large hill.

"There it is! It's the Rock Ptarmigan!" North exclaimed.

North pointed to a large bird walking on the snow. It had fluffy white feathers with splotches of charcoal grey. It had fluffy feathers all over its legs too! There was a little red strip just above each eyelid.

North flew to the bird.

"Hello! We are the Frost Wings under the command of the Arctic Fairy Queen," she said. "We hope you can help us!"

CHAPTER 9
CLOUDY

"The Arctic Fairy Queen?!" replied a very surprised bird. "Well, call me a snow-capped buttercup! I have heard many tales about the Arctic Fairy Queen. But I have never seen a fairy with my own eyes before!"

The bird extended his wing toward the fairies. "I am happy to meet you. My name is Cloudscape Frostfeather the Fifteenth. You can call me Cloudy."

"It is good to meet you, Cloudy!" North said. "My name is North. And this is Willow." North shook Cloudy's wing with her hand.

"Will you help us get these berries to a fox pup? He is hungry and alone," North said.

"Why, blow my leg feathers, it would be my pleasure!" Cloudy said. "It's not every day that a fairy asks you for a favor!"

Cloudy picked up the bundle of berries with his talons.

"Would you like a ride?" he asked. "Hop on! I'll get you there faster than a reindeer sneeze."

The fairies were delighted by the invitation. Not only would it help them hide from Blaze, but it was also fun to be carried by a bird!

They climbed onto Cloudy's back, and away they flew.

Meanwhile, Charm and Lucy were keeping Pounce busy as they waited for the food. Lucy invented a game for them to play called Hide & Tickle.

Pounce would bury his head into his long and bushy tail while the two fairies hid in the fox's fur. Then one of the fairies would tickle him. Pounce would try to correctly guess which fairy did it.

Pounce thought it was great fun. Fairy tickles are just the right amount of tickle. And the fairies loved it too. Hiding in that warm fur was so cozy!

When Willow and Lucy arrived with Cloudy, the other fairies were still hiding in Pounce's fur.

"Time to eat!" called out North.

Pounce popped his head up at the sound of North's voice. "Did they just say food?" he asked.

"They sure did!" Lucy exclaimed.

"Hooray!" cheered Charm.

Charm and Lucy flew out to welcome the fairies back and to meet the new bird friend they had made.

Cloudy flew to where Pounce was waiting. He carefully set the bundle down on the ground nearby.

Charm untied the handkerchief. Pounce's eyes grew big at the sight of the beautiful pile of berries. He quickly gobbled them up.

"Wow! He eats even faster than my Grandma!" said Cloudy. "And I thought no one could eat faster than she can."

North laughed. "Well, as you can see, Pounce was hungry!" she said. "Thank you for your help, Cloudy."

"It was my pleasure," said Cloudy. "I can't wait to tell my sister that I met fairies today. She'll be more surprised than a wet lemming!"

And then Cloudy flew away.

As Willow watched him fly into the sky, she could see the sun was almost down. She was worried they could be stranded in the dark.

CHAPTER 10
A PLAN

"We need a plan for getting Pounce home before dark," Willow said.

They all looked at one another, trying to think of a plan.

Then North spotted something fearful. "Oh no! I see a large animal in the water swimming toward us! I think it's a polar bear!"

Lucy wanted Pounce to stay hidden from the polar bear. She knew that Pounce might look like a good meal to him. She also didn't want Pounce to see the polar bear. Pounce might get scared and start barking.

Lucy had an idea for how to keep Pounce hidden with his eyes closed.

"Hey, Pounce!" Lucy said. "Let's play Hide & Tickle again! You wrap yourself up in your tail and close your eyes. But this time, I'm going to count to twenty! Don't look up until I say twenty, okay?"

Pounce agreed to play. He wrapped his big bushy tail around his body. He closed his eyes and tucked his head under his tail.

Lucy guessed it might take about twenty seconds for the polar bear to swim by them.

"Remember, Pounce. Don't look up until I say *twenty*," Lucy said.

"Okay!" Pounce replied.

Lucy began to count slowly out loud. "1 ... 2 ... 3 ..."

While Lucy counted, the other fairies huddled together to talk.

"We need a way to distract the polar bear," said North. "He must not see the fox as he swims by."

As she spoke, a gust of wind picked up and blew into their faces.

The biting cold on North's cheeks gave her an idea. She remembered how earlier in the day, the ice crystals in her eyes nearly blinded her. She turned to Willow.

"Willow, can you send an icy blast to the polar bear's eyes?" North asked. "That might blind him long enough to swim by without noticing Pounce!"

"Great idea!" said Willow.

"Oh no, my handkerchief is still out there!" exclaimed Charm.

Charm suddenly realized that her bright red handkerchief was spread out on the snow. The bear would see something that bright red against the ice, no matter how much snow was in his face!

"4 ... 5 ... 6 ..." Lucy continued to count out loud for Pounce.

The polar bear was getting closer and closer.

CHAPTER 11
THE HANDKERCHIEF

Charm flew over to the handkerchief. As soon as she picked up the corner of it, she had an idea.

She quickly began to twist the handkerchief into a skinny rope. She just kept twisting and twisting and pulling and pulling on it. The rope magically grew longer and longer.

"What are you doing?!" called Willow. "We don't have much more time before the polar bear gets here!"

"7 ... 8 ... 9 ..." continued Lucy.

"I am making a rope!" Charm called back. "If I can tie this to the ankle of the polar bear, maybe he can pull us to the shore! He certainly is big and strong enough!"

"Okay, but we better go now!" called Willow.

"10 ... 11 ... 12 ..." Lucy counted. Lucy was getting more nervous as the seconds passed by. She could see that the polar bear was getting closer.

Willow flew to the eyes of the polar bear. She cast her spell.

Snowflake crystals. Icy flurry.
Create a snowstorm in a hurry!

A flurry of snow swirled in a cloud and landed across the polar bear's face. It filled his eyes with snow. He shook his head around in response to the sudden blast of snow in his eyes.

Charm gave one end of the rope to Lucy. "Hold this," Charm whispered. "See if you can find a way to attach it to the ice floe."

"Okay," Lucy replied. "I'll try to think of something."

Then Charm quickly flew over to the polar bear's back paws. She dove into the icy cold water to get to his ankle. She swam around his paws and tried not to get hit by one of his powerful swim kicks.

It was hard to use her cold hands. They were getting stiff from the icy water. But she managed to tie a loose knot around the polar bear's ankle amid the splashing and kicking.

But just as she tried to tighten the knot that she made, the polar bear's paw hit her hard. She flew back, dropping the end of the rope.

CHAPTER 12

IN THE WATER

North saw what happened to Charm. North flew to the knot that Charm had started. She tightened it hard around the polar bear's ankle.

Then North quickly swam over to Charm, who was floating in the water. Charm was stunned and dizzy from the polar bear's kick.

North held Charm with one arm as she swam her back to the ice floe.

North was dripping wet and shivering with cold. She walked Charm, who was equally wet and cold, into the warmth of Pounce's tail.

"Can I look now?" asked Pounce from under his tail.

"Not yet!" said Lucy.

The polar bear was now only a short distance away. Lucy was trying hard to sound calm even though the bear was now terribly close. "Keep your eyes closed a little longer, Pounce. Then you can guess. 16 ... 17 ... 18 ..."

The ice crystals were forming on the bear's eyes. He was no stranger to blizzard conditions. He just kept swimming toward the shore, despite the fact he could hardly see.

He swam alongside the ice floe as the fairies nervously held their breath.

And then the polar bear swam past them.

The fairies let out a huge sigh of relief.

"Twenty!" called out Lucy.

When Pounce popped his head up, Lucy quickly shoved the end of the rope into his mouth. She hoped this would trigger his play instincts.

She was right. As soon as the rope was in his mouth, Pounce gripped his teeth tightly around it with a playful growl.

"Hold onto the rope, Pounce!" instructed Lucy. "We need that polar bear to pull our little iceberg back home! Dig your paws into that hole so you won't slip!"

CHAPTER 13
HOLDING ON

Pounce dug his paws into the hole he had dug out earlier. He held onto the rope with his teeth.

The rope was still firmly tied around the polar bear's ankle. It stretched out as the bear continued to swim away from them.

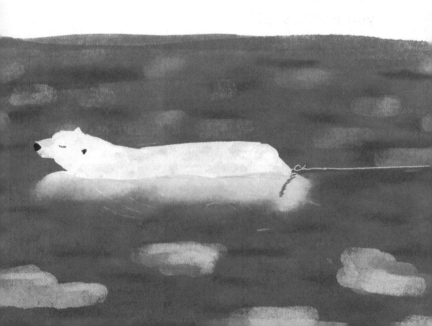

The ice floe was moving! It was being pulled by the polar bear as he swam. The fairies cheered. "It's working! Keep going, Pounce! Hold on a little longer!" said Lucy.

As they glided across the water, Lucy turned to Charm. She saw that Charm was badly hurt from the polar bear kick.

Lucy was the team's Healer. But so far, she had only used her powers for minor scratches and bruises. Charm took such a big hit from the polar bear paw. *Will my healing powers be strong enough?* she wondered.

Lucy sat next to Charm. "I'm going to try to help you," she said. And then she began to sing a gentle and beautiful song.

May your heart be comforted
From injuries that take their toll.
May a healing warmth embrace you
And make your broken parts whole.

As Lucy sang, she rubbed her hands together. Bright, golden sparks rose from her hands. They filled the air and surrounded Charm, bathing her in a glowing, golden light.

A warmth traveled throughout Charm's whole body. Her cheeks started to show some pink again.

Charm opened her eyes and smiled at all the beautiful light around her. She sat up slowly with a big smile. "Thank you, Lucy!" she said. "I feel so much better now!"

"It was my pleasure," said Lucy. "You were so brave out there." And then she gave Charm a big hug.

Just a little while later, the polar bear reached the shore. He lumbered out of the sea, pulling the ice floe onto the shore.

Lucy whispered to Pounce. "Let's wait right here until we don't see the polar bear anymore." The fairies watched the polar bear walk away.

Charm wanted to retrieve her rope that was still tied to the polar bear's ankle. But that might make him turn around. Then he would see Pounce. It was too big of a risk to take.

So, the polar bear dragged the rope behind him. He walked away, leaving big footprints in the snow.

CHAPTER 14
ALMOST HOME

Once he was gone, Pounce bounded off the ice floe and onto the shore. The fairies followed.

"Now we just need to find Pounce's parents," Willow said. "North and I spotted fox dens not far from here. Maybe we'll find his parents there."

"I know the way to that spot," North said. "Follow me!"

As they traveled across the shore toward the dens, the crow once again flew overhead. But this time, there was no time to hide.

The crow landed right in front of
the fairies and the fox. Blaze jumped
off its back.

She stood in front of the fairies with
her hands on her hips. She had Charm's
rope hanging off her waist.

She made a sharp and shrill whistle. Several fairy minions buzzed over. Just like the crow, the minion fairies had red wings and red eyes. They looked like they were in a trance.

"Didn't you learn how to clean up after yourselves?" Blaze sneered. "I knew you must be close when I saw the red rope trailing off the polar bear's leg. It was easy enough to follow his jumbo footprints back to you."

Then Blaze held up Charm's magic rope that was hanging on her side. "Thanks for the present," she smirked.

Pounce grew agitated and began barking loudly.

In the distance, two worried Arctic foxes heard this barking. It was just the sound they wanted to hear. They ran toward the sound.

"Pounce!" they called.

"Mom! Dad!" Pounce cried, as he ran toward them.

Pounce and his parents were reunited. They joyfully nuzzled their faces together.

But it wasn't long before Pounce remembered that his new fairy friends were in danger. He ran back toward the fairies. His parents followed him.

Pounce began yelping at Blaze and her minions again. This time, his parents joined in. The three barking foxes were quite a frightening sight! Blaze knew it was time to retreat.

"Minions, let's go!" Blaze commanded. "We'll be back another day!" And with that, she jumped on her red crow, and they flew away.

Willow turned to the Arctic fox family. "Thank you so much for scaring them away!"

"Oh, thank you," said Pounce's mother. "We were so worried. We looked everywhere for Pounce. We did not know what had happened to him."

"He was stuck on an ice floe that had floated out to sea," explained Lucy. "But we all worked together to get the ice floe back to shore."

"Thank you, fairies! What a relief it is to have you home, Pounce!" said Pounce's father.

"Pounce, now it is time for us to go home. We promise to visit you again someday," said Lucy.

The fairies gathered around Pounce and gave him one big hug all at once.

Then the Frost Wings said goodbye and flew away.

CHAPTER 15
A WISH

Just as the sun was setting, the fairies arrived home. Using her fairy magic, the queen had made the Frost Wings home cozy and beautiful.

Dried flower garlands were draped across the ceilings. Star-shaped lamps were filled with glowing glitter.

Chairs, tables, and beds were made with twisted twigs of willow. They were topped with soft pillows of springy moss and warm blankets made of musk oxen fur.

Willow and North sat at the table talking over some tea. Lucy sat in her favorite reading chair with a book.

Charm looked out of the window. She couldn't stop thinking about her magic rope. She wanted to find a way to get it back. Then she saw the first twinkling star of the night sky.

She made a wish. "I really want to get my magic rope back!"

Read the Next
Frost Wings Adventure!

Will Charm get her magic
rope back from Blaze?

Will the Frost Wings get
their new Arctic friends to
Puffin Beak Mountain through
a winter blizzard?

LUCY'S ANIMAL NOTES

Arctic Fox

❄ In the winter, an Arctic fox's fur is white to match the snow. In the summer, their fur changes to brown to match the ground.

❄ They use the same family dens for many years.

❄ They prefer to eat small rodents called lemmings. But if they are very hungry, they will eat what they can find, including insects and berries.

❄ Their babies are called pups or kits.

Rock Ptarmigan

❄ Ptarmigan is pronounced *tar-mi-gan*. The P is silent.

❄ The feathers on their legs and feet keep them warm.

❄ Their feathers are white in the winter. They change to brown and black in the summer.

❄ The male has a splash of red above its eye.

❄ They mainly eat insects. But they will also eat flowers, berries, and other plants.

❄ Although they can fly, they walk on the ground most of the time.

Polar Bear

❉ Polar bears are excellent swimmers. They can swim for many hours to get from one piece of ice to another.

❉ Their fur isn't white. Surprisingly, it is transparent. The fur has a hollow core that reflects light.

❉ Beneath their thick fur, they have black skin. This helps them soak up the sun's rays to keep warm.

❉ Polar bear cubs will stay with their mother for about two years. During this time, they learn the skills they need to live in the Arctic.

THE FROST WINGS SERIES

THANK YOU

Dear Reader,

Thank you for reading the first Frost Wings adventure! I really hope you enjoyed it.

If you liked this book, please leave a review on Amazon.com. I would love to hear what you think! And please write your answer to this question:

What is your favorite animal?

Thank you!
- Marisa

ABOUT THE AUTHOR

Marisa Peña lives in Washington state with her husband, two children, and a very sweet kitty cat named Mochi.

Along with writing and drawing, she loves spending time with her family, growing food, and running on trails in the woods.

Marisa is also a board game inventor. She has co-invented dozens of award-winning board games for kids and families, including *Outfoxed!*, *Dinosaur Escape*, and *The Fairy Game*. You can see all her games at: www.departmentofrec.com.

Made in United States
Troutdale, OR
03/19/2024